fimbles

Blue

The Fimbles were playing hide-and-seek. Baby Pom put her hands over her eyes, squeaking with excitement. She loved this game.

"I'll hide first," said Fimbo. "Start counting!"

"One, two, three," began Florrie, as she closed her eyes.

"Fimbo hide!" Pom giggled, squeezing her eyes shut.

When Fimbo was sure they weren't looking, he rushed away from the Purple Meadow to hide.

But Fimbo soon stopped running. His fingers began to twinkle and his nose began to twitch.

"Oh, I'm getting the Fimbling Feeling!" he said.

The branches of the Tinkling Tree began to shimmer, and its flowers began to tinkle.

The bubbles from the Bubble Fall went "Ping! Ping!" as they popped.

Fimbo began to dance and sing.

"I can feel a twinkling,
I can hear a sound,
It's telling me there's something
Waiting to be found!
Where is it? Where is it?
What could it be?
I think it might be over there,
Let's go and see!"

Fimbo twirled round and round, coming to a stop in the Playdips. "Hmm! I can't see anything," he said. Just then, he saw something sparkling and shimmering in the Funpuddle. "Ooh! What's that?"

Fimbo went over to the
Funpuddle and peered at it.
"It's not a puddle – it's
blue!" he said.

Fimbo picked up a stick and carefully dipped it into the blue.

"Look! I've found some **blue**!" he said.

Fimbo swirled his stick in the blue.
"This is fun!" he said. "I wonder what this blue is?"
He lifted up his stick and
some of the blue dripped
onto the ground, but
Fimbo didn't notice.

"I think the others
would like to see this!
I'll go and find them."

Fimbo raced off, stepping into the blue on the floor by mistake and leaving footprints behind him.

Fimbo went to look in the Comfy Corner.
His nose began to twitch again.
"I can smell crackers," said Fimbo. "Yum, yum!
I love crackers! My favourite food!" he said.

He took a cracker out of the cracker barrel and ate it quickly. There was one cracker left.

"That cracker looks very lonely on its own," thought Fimbo. "I'd better eat that one, too."

So he did.

"Oh where can Fimbo be?" sighed Florrie.

"Look!" called Baby Pom.

Instead of finding Fimbo, Baby Pom had found something blue on the ground.

"What is it?" asked Florrie, as Rockit bounced towards them.
"A piece of the sky?" suggested Rockit.
Florrie laughed. "I think it's a footprint," she said.

"Aha!" said Rockit. "This could be the footprint of the..."

"...Blue Galoo!"

"What's a Blue Galoo?" asked Florrie.

"I don't know. But it's blue and it has big blue footprints!" answered Rockit.

Bessie flew in to see what everyone was looking at.

"What does a Blue Galoo look like, Bessie?" Florrie asked.

Bessie smiled. "If you follow the footprints, you might find out," she said.

Florrie, Baby Pom and Rockit looked
at each other.
"Find! Find!" cried Pom.
"That's a good idea," said Florrie.
"Let's follow the blue footprints to
see if they lead us to the Blue Galoo!"

Rockit was excited about going to find the Blue Galoo – but he didn't want to go first. He hopped along after Florrie and Pom.

So Florrie, Baby Pom and Rockit followed the trail of blue footprints away from the Funpuddle. They had forgotten all about looking for Fimbo.

They followed the blue footprints all the way to the Comfy Corner.

Florrie saw the empty cracker barrel.
"Look, the Blue Galoo has been here, and he's eaten up all our crackers!" she said.

Fimbo was looking for the others. Without knowing it, he had now walked in a big circle, and was back at the Funpuddle.

"Where can everyone be?" thought Fimbo. Just then he saw the blue footprints on the ground.

"Look at those! They're blue!"

He started to walk round the Playdips when suddenly...bump!
Florrie, Baby Pom and Rockit, who were still following the
footprints, bumped into Fimbo, making him jump in surprise.

"You! You! Blue Galoo!" said Baby Pom, excitedly –
pointing at Fimbo's feet.

"What's a Blue Galoo?" asked Fimbo.

"You! You!" squeaked Baby Pom.

Fimbo looked down at his feet and started to laugh.

"I'm a Blue Galoo!" he giggled. "I found some blue in the Funpuddle," he explained. "I must have dropped some of it on the ground and stepped in it. My feet made these blue footprints!"

"Oh, so it was you who ate up all the crackers!" said Florrie, laughing.

"I'm sorry, Florrie. I was hungry and there were only two left," Fimbo explained.

"I wonder what a real Blue Galoo looks like," said Florrie.
Roly Mo popped out of his hole to answer the question.
"I think a Blue Galoo looks like whatever you want it to look like."

Fimbo nodded. "Look," he said. Everyone watched as he poked his paintbrush into the Funpuddle, then dropped a blob of blue onto a piece of paper. He folded the paper in half.

"There!" said Fimbo, opening the paper.
"What's that, Fimbo?" asked Rockit.
"It's my Blue Galoo! My very own Blue Galoo!" said Fimbo, laughing.

"What would your Blue Galoo
look like, Florrie?" Bessie asked.

"It would look like a big blue flower!" answered Florrie, excitedly.

"Blue, blue!" squeaked Baby Pom.

"Big blue stripes!" shouted Rockit, jumping up and down.

"Definitely a blue book!" said Roly Mo.

"What about you, Bessie?" asked Fimbo.

"I think my Blue Galoo would be a different blue thing every day!" said Bessie, with a giggle.